AMAZING GRACE

Babette Douglas

Illustrated by
Barry Rockwell

Kiss a me™ ❤
Productions

Kiss A Me™ Productions, Inc. produces toys and booklets for children with an emphasis on love and learning. For more information on how to purchase a Kiss A Me collectible and plush toy or to receive information on additional Kiss A Me products, write or call:

Kiss a me™ Pro uctions

Kiss A Me Productions, Inc.
90 Garfield Ave.
Sayville, NY 11782
888 - KISSAME
888-547-7263

About the Kiss A Me Teacher Creature Series:
This delightfully illustrated series of inspirational books by
Babette Douglas has won praise from parents and educators alike.
Through her wonderful "teacher creatures" she imparts profound lessons of tolerance
and responsible living with heartwarming insights and a humorous touch.

AMAZING GRACE

Written by Babette Douglas
Illustrated by Barry Rockwell

ISBN 1-89034-333-1
Printed in China

www.kissame.com

To *Theresa M. Santmann,*
Who lives with "amazing grace"

Preface

In our wonderful and ever-changing world,
children are our greatest legacy
and investment in the future.
And yet, in the world we have prepared
for them, love seems to have been mislaid.

With this little story, one little creature,
Grace, seems to have found love again
and put it into action.

With an unshakable belief in kindness,
hope for a brighter future and a loving desire
to make a difference, Grace teaches us all...
that everyone can.

Grace, when she opened her eyes,
Was the youngest dolphin at sea.
She could hardly believe the wonder
Of our world and all it can be.

When first she rose to the surface
For a breath of refreshing air,
With joy she admired the sky,
The sun, and the clouds everywhere.

She loved the cool blue water
That was her home deep in the sea.
She enjoyed the rolling waves
As she tumbled joyous and free.

She swam with octopus creatures,
Sea turtles, jelly fish and eels.
She'd tickle whales that were passing
And tug on tails of the seals.

She taught herself to juggle,
And up to the surface she'd go,
Where she'd toss high the starfish
She found in the ocean below.

But as Grace traveled the oceans,
She noticed **things out of place.**
Seeing land debris floating
Brought a frown to her face.

"This must be an error I'm viewing,
For no one would willingly trash
The home where others are living
By dumping toxic oil and ash.

"Who would willingly darken
The home of another at sea
By carelessly dumping their waste,
Trash and unhealthy debris?"

Grace began patrolling the ocean
Finding people dumping carelessly.
She saw them tossing refuse
She knew had no place in the sea.

She felt others were simply mistaken
In carelessly tossing items away.
She then decided to help them,
Returning their items without delay.

She'd circle people who were boating
(Unaware of Grace patrolling the sea),
But when a can was *carelessly dropped* –
It was returned by Grace instantly!

Grace, while swimming the ocean,
Would deliver with balance and speed.
Whatever was tossed overboard,
She viewed as an item they'd need.

Now the people fishing and boating
Were shocked by their *on-board* debris,
For items they tossed without thinking
Returned as debris from the sea.

In her haste to help and be caring,
The cans she returned with such flair
Bounced off people on board staring
At Grace as she leaped in the air.

Overboard came bottles and wrappers,
Food and cartons and cans,
Returned with tires and boxes
And trash that belonged on the land.

Grace kept cleaning the ocean
Of all things *not of the sea*.
And boaters kept dodging and ducking
To avoid being hit by debris.

Now, captains trolling the waters
Began avoiding meeting with Grace,
For none wanted garbage that's tossed
Quickly flying back to its place.

They felt a solution was needed.
"To hide from a fish is a disgrace!"
The captains finally voted
To contain trash in an appropriate place!

Now boaters happily go boating
(Grace seldom finds ocean debris).
People have finally agreed together
To stop polluting the sea.

Look for Grace whenever you're boating.
You'll find her dancing on waves,
Amazing all who are passing
And enjoying the ocean she saves.

Now...

Amazing Grace isn't a dolphin
Or a person you might chance to meet.
It's a quality used in good living
That can turn life from a trial to a treat.

THE END

Babette Douglas, a talented poet and artist, has written over 30 children's books in which diverse creatures live together in harmony, friendship and respect. She brings to her delightful stories the insights and caring accumulated in a lifetime of varied experiences.

"I believe strongly in the healing power of love," she says. "I want to empower children to see with their hearts and to love all the creatures of the earth, including themselves." The unique stories told by her "teacher creatures" enable children to learn to recognize their own gifts and to value tolerance, compassion, optimism and perseverance.

Ms. Douglas, who was born and educated in New York City, has lived in Sayville, New York for over forty years.

Additional Kiss A Me™ teacher-creature stories:

BLUE WISE

BLUFFALO Wins His Great Race

CURLY HARE

FALCON EDDIE

THE FLUTTERBY

KISS A ME: A Little Whale Watching

KISS A ME Goes to School

KISS A ME To the Rescue

LARKSPUR

THE LYON BEAR™

THE LYON BEAR™ deTails

THE LYON BEAR™: The Mane Event

MISS EVONNE And the Mice of Nice

MISS TEAK And the Endorphins

NOREEN: The Real King of the Jungle

OSCARPUS

ROSEBUD

SQUIRT: The Magic Cuddle Fish

**Character toys are available for each book.
For additional information on books, toys,
and other products visit us at:**

www.kissame.com